RED AGAIN

by **Barbara Lehman**

Houghton Mifflin Harcourt
Boston New York

For Sylvie

www.hmhco.com

The illustrations in this book were done in watercolor, gouache, and ink.

ISBN 978-0-544-81859-0

Manufactured in China
SCP 10 9 8 7 6 5 4 3 2 1
4500665322

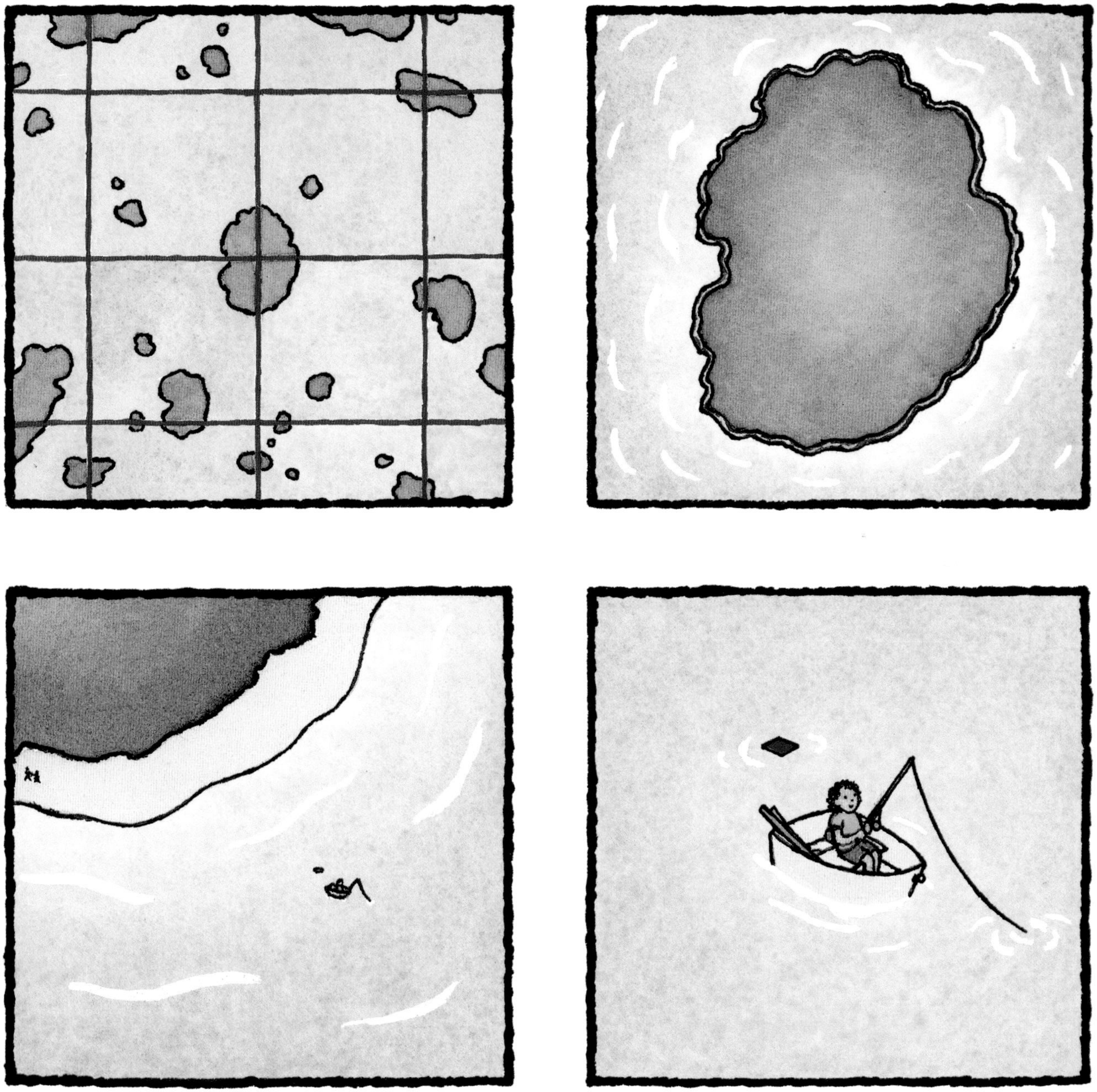

W
E